Peep!

Peep!

WITHDRAWN

Peep!

To my friends who inspire me to be brave,
and who love me whether I am or not.

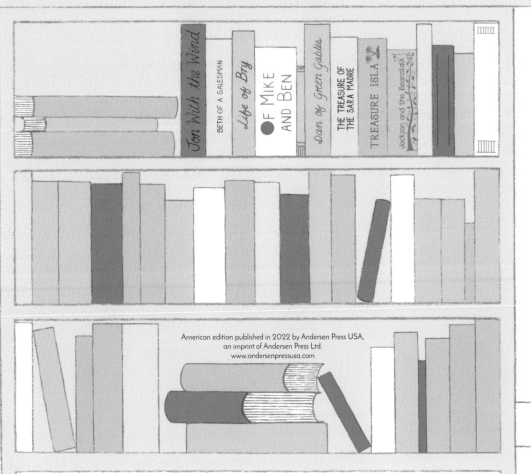

Jon With the Wind
BETH OF A SALESMAN
Life of Bry
OF MIKE AND BEN
Dan Of Green Gables
THE TREASURE OF THE SARA MADRE
TREASURE ISLA
Jackson and the Beanstalk

American edition published in 2022 by Andersen Press USA,
an imprint of Andersen Press Ltd.
www.andersenpressusa.com

First published in Great Britain in 2021 by Andersen Press Ltd., 20 Vauxhall Bridge Road, London SW1V 2SA

Text and illustrations copyright © Meg McLaren 2021

Distributed in the United States and Canada by
Lerner Publishing Group, Inc.
241 First Avenue North
Minneapolis, MN 55401 USA

For reading levels and more information, look up this title at www.lernerbooks.com.

Library of Congress Cataloging-in-Publication Data Available
ISBN 978-1-7284-6771-9
1-TOPPAN-04/01/22

MEG McLAREN

PEEP!

Andersen Press USA

Dot was not
like other dogs.

Peep!
Peep!

While the other dogs headed to the park,
Dot preferred to stay at home with Peep.

Home was the safest,
coziest place Dot knew.

It was almost perfect. Only Mail
and Bath got in the way.

Peep helped Dot to take
care of Mail. . .

but no one could escape Bath.

Peep encouraged Dot to do the things other dogs like to do.

FETCH, DOT!

But if Dot didn't feel like it, Peep stuck with her.

They were best friends.

Peep!
Peep!

Their favorite place was the garden, and together
they patrolled it daily. Sometimes there were
strange smells or surprises. . .

but it wasn't too scary
because Peep always went first.

Peep!

Peep!
Peep!
Peep!

Once they'd made sure the garden was safe,
Dot could relax knowing that all was well.

yawn...

Until one day, it wasn't.

Peep! Peep!

Dot didn't know what
to do. Peep had never gone
off on his own before!

But then Dot spotted him.

She couldn't let Peep
face the park alone.
Dot had to get him back.

But Peep wasn't alone.

ROOOOOW!

And before Dot
knew it. . .

Peep! Peep!

Peep was gone again!

Peep!
Peep!
Peep!

Peep! Peep! Peep!

Peep and the other dogs were
having so much fun, they
didn't notice. . .

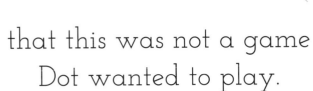

that this was not a game
Dot wanted to play.

Then things got even worse.

The big dog came over

and would not leave.

No matter how fast Dot ran, Big Dog was always right behind, and Peep was out of reach.

Peep! Peep!

Dot darted and weaved, and as her paws tore through the grass she realized. . .

Peeeep!

Peep!

. . . that she and Peep were having fun!

At last Peep and Dot were back together.
Big Dog was so glad he could make up
for all the trouble he had caused.

But then Dot had a horrible thought: what if one of these other dogs took Peep again?

Dot decided they needed to go home. Even the garden wasn't safe any more.

They didn't go out the next day or the day after that.

Until Dot woke up to a garden full of unusual sounds.

arf!

squeee

TOOT!

wheeze

squeee

CREAK!

arf!

All of the dogs had a
Peep of their very own,
and they'd brought
them to play!

Peep!

wheeze

CRACK!

Dot still loved staying at home with Peep. . .

Peep!
Peep!